Dear Parent:
Your child's love of reading starts here!

Every child learns to read in a different way and at his or her own speed. You can help your young reader improve and become more confident by encouraging his or her own interests and abilities. You can also guide your child's spiritual development by reading stories with biblical values and Bible stories, like I Can Read! books published by Zonderkidz. From books your child reads with you to the first books he or she reads alone, there are I Can Read! books for every stage of reading:

SHARED READING
Basic language, word repetition, and whimsical illustrations, ideal for sharing with your emergent reader.

BEGINNING READING
Short sentences, familiar words, and simple concepts for children eager to read on their own.

READING WITH HELP
Engaging stories, longer sentences, and language play for developing readers.

READING ALONE
Complex plots, challenging vocabulary, and high-interest topics for the independent reader.

ADVANCED READING
Short paragraphs, chapters, and exciting themes for the perfect bridge to chapter books.

I Can Read! books have introduced children to the joy of reading since 1957. Featuring award-winning authors and illustrators and a fabulous cast of beloved characters, I Can Read! books set the standard for beginning readers.

A lifetime of discovery begins with the magical words "I Can Read!"

Visit www.icanread.com for information on enriching your child's reading experience.
Visit www.zonderkidz.com for more Zonderkidz I Can Read! titles.

(Love) is not rude.
—*1 Corinthians 13:5*

ZONDERKIDZ

Troo's Secret Clubhouse
Copyright © 2011 by Cheryl Crouch
Illustrations copyright © 2011 by Kevin Zimmer

Requests for information should be addressed to:
Zonderkidz, *Grand Rapids, Michigan 49530*

Library of Congress Cataloging-in-Publication Data

Crouch, Cheryl, 1968-
    Troo's secret clubhouse / story by Cheryl Crouch ; pictures by Kevin
Zimmer.
        p. cm. — (I can read! level 2) (Rainforest animals)
     ISBN 978-0-310-71809-3 (softcover)
     [1. Brothers and sisters—Fiction. 2. Tree kangaroos—Fiction. 3. Kangaroos—
Fiction. 4. Rain forest animals—Fiction. 5. Christian life—Fiction.] I. Zimmer, Kevin,
ill. II. Title.
    PZ7.C8838Ts 2010
    [E]—dc22
    {B}   2009037515

Editor: Mary Hassinger
Art direction & design: Jody Langley

Printed in China

11 12 13 14 15 /SCC/ 10 9 8 7 6 5 4 3 2

RAINFOREST FRIENDS
TROO'S SECRET CLUBHOUSE

story by Cheryl Crouch

pictures by Kevin Zimmer

Troo panted and lay down
on the wooden floor
of the clubhouse.
Getting Rilla up the ladder
was hard work.

"You have to learn to climb,"
Troo told little Rilla.
"Keewa and I can't carry you
up forever."
"But I am a water rat!" Rilla said.
"I told you to build
our clubhouse on the ground!"

Keewa shook his head.

"A supersecret clubhouse

is much better high in the air.

No one can see us

or hear our secret plans here."

Troo's little sister Meri stuck

her head up through the trapdoor.

"What secret plans?" she asked.

Rilla rolled her eyes and said,

"I guess they aren't so secret now."

Keewa frowned at Troo.

"Did you invite your baby sister

to our clubhouse?"

"No!" Troo said.

"She must have followed me."

Troo yelled at Meri, "Go home!

We don't want babies in our fort."

Meri's big eyes filled with tears.

"I am not a baby," she said.

"Why can't I play?"

"We don't play," Troo said.

"We do big, important things,
   but we can't tell you about them.
You are too little to understand."

Meri went down.

Troo could hear Meri crying
all the way down the ladder.

"Okay," Troo said, "she's gone.
Let's make a plan."

Keewa asked, "What kind of plan?
I can't think of anything big
or important."

"I have to go anyway," Rilla said.

"It's time to catch fish for lunch."

"What?" said Troo.

"We just got you up!"

Keewa started for the trapdoor.

"And I have to find bugs

for my bug collection."

"Fine," said Troo.

"Let's carry Rilla down.

Then I'll help you with your bugs."

"No, thanks," Keewa said.
"Remember how you ate
my leaf collection?"

Troo carried Rilla down.

Troo climbed back up the ladder.

In the clubhouse, it was very still

and quiet and lonely.

Too lonely.

Troo missed his friends.

He even missed Meri!

He wondered what his little

sister was doing.

Troo went down the ladder
and snuck through the rainforest
to look for Meri.
Troo found her at his favorite bush,
nibbling tasty leaves.
He wanted to ask Meri to share.

Then he remembered the mean words
he had said to her.
Why should she share with him?

Troo waited until Meri left.

He chewed a few leaves.

They didn't taste sweet today.

His tummy hurt.

A happy sound made Troo look up.

He peeked through the huge leaves.

Meri and her friends flew past,

laughing and yelling.

They swung from tree to tree,

playing Troo's favorite game.

Troo didn't want to be alone.

"I want to play!" he called.

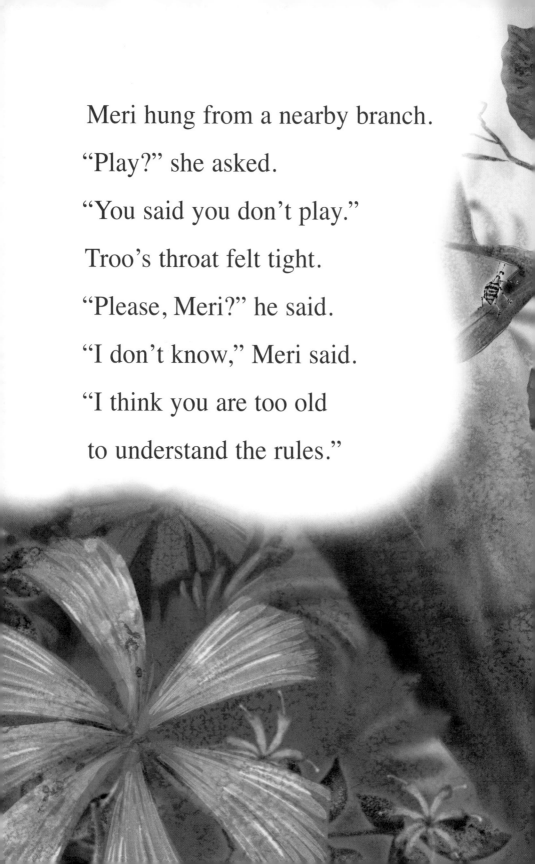

Meri hung from a nearby branch.

"Play?" she asked.

"You said you don't play."

Troo's throat felt tight.

"Please, Meri?" he said.

"I don't know," Meri said.

"I think you are too old

to understand the rules."

"What rules?" Troo asked.

"We just have fun," Meri answered.

"And we don't do anything big
or important like you do."

Troo saw the others glide by.

He wanted to glide with them.

"It's no fun to be left out,"
Troo said.

Meri agreed, "It stinks."

Troo climbed over and hung by Meri.

"I am sorry I was mean," Troo said.

"The Bible says love is never rude."

"Even to little sisters?" Meri asked.

"Even to little sisters," Troo said.

"I forgive you, big brother,"

Meri said at last.

She smiled.

"And I guess you can play with us,

as long as you remember the rules!"

"First rule: have fun!" Troo shouted.

He leaped for the next tree.

Meri jumped past him.

"Next rule: be nice to your sister,"
Meri yelled.

"I don't know," Troo said.

"That sounds kind of big
and important to me."

Meri

Troo's little sister who can leap thirty feet without getting hurt.

Troo

A tree kangaroo with claws and a tail that help him move more easily in trees than on land.

Lipstick Plant

The lipstick plant has bright red flowers that look like lipstick and they love hot, rainforest weather.

Rilla

A water rat who is comfortable on land and in water.

Keewa

A cuscus who looks a bit like a possum and moves slowly, like a sloth.